ARTIST'S NOTE

It's an honor to illustrate this classic Christmas poem written by Clement C. Moore nearly two hundred years ago. As I reread it, I was reminded of how beautifully it was written and how its words are so familiar to our lives at Christmastime.

I've never seen St. Nick in person myself, and as I painted these pictures, I couldn't help but wonder what he'd think of how I was drawing him. I took some visual clues directly from the famous text—"miniature sleigh," "eight tiny reindeer," and "a little old driver"—and I created a more diminutive St. Nick and reindeer.

Christmas brings joy and love all over the world—no matter who we are, where we live, or how we celebrate. That's what I wanted to portray in this book—one magical Christmas Eve celebrated by children from different kinds of families. I hope you enjoy meeting all of them.

LOREN LONG

THE NIGHT BEFORE CHRISTMAS

BY CLEMENT C. MOORE
PICTURES BY LOREN LONG

HARPER
An Imprint of HarperCollinsPublishers

'Twas the night before Christmas, when all through the house
Not a creature was stirring, not even a mouse.

The stockings were hung by the chimney with care,
In hopes that St. Nicholas soon would be there.

The children were nestled all snug in their beds,
While visions of sugarplums danced in their heads;

And Mama in her kerchief and I in my cap

Had just settled down for a long winter's nap —

When out on the lawn there arose such a clatter,
I sprang from the bed to see what was the matter.

Away to the window I flew like a flash,
Tore open the shutters, and threw up the sash.

The moon on the breast of the new-fallen snow
Gave the luster of midday to objects below;

When, what to my wondering eyes should appear,
But a miniature sleigh, and eight tiny reindeer,

With a little old driver so lively and quick,
I knew in a moment it must be St. Nick.

More rapid than eagles his coursers they came,
And he whistled, and shouted, and called them by name:

"Now, Dasher! Now, Dancer! Now, Prancer and Vixen!
On, Comet! On, Cupid! On, Donder and Blitzen!"

"To the top of the porch! To the top of the wall!
Now dash away! Dash away! Dash away all!"

As dry leaves that before the wild hurricane fly,
When they meet with an obstacle, mount to the sky;

So up to the housetop the coursers they flew,
With the sleigh full of toys, and St. Nicholas too.

And then, in a twinkling, I heard on the roof
The prancing and pawing of each little hoof.

As I drew in my head and was turning around,
Down the chimney St. Nicholas came with a bound.

He was dressed all in fur, from his head to his foot,
And his clothes were all tarnished with ashes and soot;

A bundle of toys he had flung on his back,
And he looked like a peddler just opening his pack.

His eyes, how they twinkled!
His dimples, how merry!
His cheeks were like roses,
    his nose like a cherry;

His droll little mouth was drawn
    up like a bow,
And the beard of his chin was
    as white as the snow.

The stump of a pipe he held tight in his teeth,
And the smoke it encircled his head like a wreath;

He had a broad face, and a little round belly
That shook, when he laughed, like a bowlful of jelly.

He was chubby and plump,
   a right jolly old elf,
And I laughed when I saw him
   in spite of myself.
A wink of his eye and a twist
   of his head
Soon gave me to know I had
   nothing to dread.

He spoke not a word,
  but went straight
  to his work,
And filled all the stockings,
  then turned with a jerk,

And laying his finger aside of his nose,
And giving a nod, up the chimney he rose.

He sprang to his sleigh, to his team gave a whistle,
And away they all flew like the down of a thistle.

But I heard him exclaim,
ere he drove out of sight,

"Merry Christmas to all

To Griffith and Graham
—L.L.

The Night Before Christmas
Illustrations copyright © 2020 by Loren Long
All rights reserved. Manufactured in China.
No part of this book may be used or reproduced in any manner whatsoever
without written permission except in the case of brief quotations embodied in
critical articles and reviews.
For information address HarperCollins Children's Books,
a division of HarperCollins Publishers, 195 Broadway, New York, NY 10007.
www.harpercollinschildrens.com

Library of Congress Control Number: 2019951149
ISBN 978-0-06-286946-3

The artist used acrylic paint and colored pencil to create the illustrations
for this book.
Designed by Jeanne L. Hogle
20 21 22 23 24 SCP 10 9 8 7 6 5 4 3 2 1
❖
First Edition